Let's Talk About Feelings

All My Feelings At Preschool

Nathan's Day

T0116752

Foreword by David W. Krueger, M.D., F.A.P.A.

Written by Susan Conlin, M.Ed. and Susan Levine Friedman, M.S.W.
Illustrated by M. Kathryn Smith

Parenting Press, Inc.
Seattle, WA

Acknowledgements

Dedicated to our children—Judith, Daniel, Aaron, and Eli.

Cover Design by Alice C. Merrill
Book Design by Nancy Campbell

Copyright © 1991, Parenting Press, Inc.

Originally published as *Nathan's Day at Preschool*

First printing 1991

ISBN 0-943990-60-2 Paper
ISBN 0-943990-61-0 Library binding
LC 90-62679

Parenting Press, Inc.
P.O. Box 75267
Seattle, WA 98125

Introduction

Many of our children spend a significant amount of time in daycare centers, family childcare homes, and in preschool or kindergarten. Nurturing our children can be, by far, one of the most challenging and rewarding jobs entrusted to adults.

The task of choosing a caregiver can be overwhelming: Will my child be safe? How will s/he feel there? How will the caregiver's personality and values interact with my child's? How will the caregiver respond to my child's emotional and psychological needs? What will the other children be like?

Parents trying to juggle work lives and home lives often believe that one or the other suffers and feel guilty. Both children and parents may struggle with separation anxiety. Caregivers have the tremendous job of helping each child feel special while juggling the business of childcare and family dynamics.

We can work together. We need to talk about how we feel and encourage our children to do the same. We need strategies to deal with sensitive areas—separation and transition times, conflicts, hurt feelings, and special needs. And we need to recognize and encourage caregivers whose primary concern is our children's emotional well being.

This book can be used in two ways. You can read it as a story —beginning to end—all in one sitting. Or feel free to read just one page of *Nathan's Day* per day and talk about that feeling with your child(ren). Sometimes it's better to begin slowly. You can gauge the attention span available for new ideas and adjust your reading accordingly. You might also use the book as a springboard for your own questions and solutions.

We hope *Nathan's Day* will reflect a common experience and add to your own ideas and hopes for the children you care about.

Here's to the challenge!

Susan & Susan

Foreword

From the first days and weeks of life, the most basic desires we have as human beings are to connect with those important to us, to communicate and to feel understood, and to experience mastery. Perhaps what our children and we *most* need to understand is our feelings.

The majority of adolescents and adults I see in psychotherapy have never accurately experienced nor fully expressed their own feelings.

For the small child, who still thinks concretely, such abstract concepts as feelings are not easy to grasp. Feelings aren't tangible, visible, or three-dimensional. You can't put feelings on the table and look at them.

So how can you teach children to recognize and talk about feelings? You've already taken a few first steps: you've decided children's feelings matter and you care enough to have bought this book.

Let Nathan and his buddies take it from here. They will lead you and your child through basic feelings and issues. The authors masterfully weave Nathan's experiences with questions to start discussion. Together you will cross a bridge from Nathan's feelings to your child's own experience—shared and affirmed together.

Books help children learn and make new discoveries. For the small child, the world of feelings can be a confusing, yet exciting, new territory to explore. As adults, it is our great privilege to share in that new experience.

Entertaining and instructive, this is a "sit on my lap and let's talk about it" book. *Nathan's Day* will help bring into focus feelings about common, yet confusing, situations and experiences. Children can come to better understand and express their emotions through talking about their experiences and feelings as prompted by the story.

Adults can answer the questions too. Reading together and answering the questions on each page offers you an active reading experience. The authors engage, even require, communication and interaction about feelings. With this book, children can move from confusion about feelings as a private experience to discussing them openly and clearly with a caring adult.

Empathy is not a gift. It is a hard-work miracle. Nathan helps us in our quest to empathetically enter the internal world of the child, and to look at the world through his or her eyes.

David W. Krueger
Dr. Krueger is a psychiatrist and psychoanalyst,
and is the author of eight books; the latest is
What Is A Feeling?

Hi, my name is Nathan. I usually like snuggling with my bear Alfie in the morning. But today I remembered about a picture I was making at my school. It was going to be a surprise for my mom!

CAPABLE

I jumped out of bed, pulled off my pajamas and put on my new overalls with the silver snaps. I can get dressed almost by myself!

"Breakfast, Nathan!" I heard Dad calling me.

I gave Alfie a hug and ran downstairs. Mmmmmm. I could smell cinnamon toast.

What can you do all by yourself?

I feel capable.

MIXED FEELINGS

When we got to my school, Mom helped me take off my boots. I put my blanket away. At first I was happy to be at my school—Kids' Place. But then I started to feel sad. I didn't want to stay. I felt a little scared.

"Can you stay here, Mom?" I asked.

"That would be fun, but I need to go straight to my class and then to work," Mom explained. "But I'll stay for a few minutes. Would that help?"

My teacher Jackie saw me. She came over and smiled. "I'm glad you're here, Nathan. Why don't you show your mom how you fixed up your cubby last week?"

I felt happy again. Mom calls that having mixed feelings. First I felt sad, but then I felt happy to be at Kids' Place.

Tell about a time when you felt mixed up.

I feel mixed up.

COOPERATIVE

I saw my friend Max at the art table. "I know!" I thought. "I can work on my picture for Mom."

Max and I shared the glue. Then Mandy came over and grabbed it.

"Hey!" I yelled. "That's our glue! Give it back!"

"I need it for my feathers!" Mandy yelled back. "You have to share."

Jackie came over. "Looks like we have a problem," she said. "One glue and three children. What can we do so everyone gets what they need?"

"They could wait till I'm done," said Mandy.

"Well, we could take turns," I said, even though I didn't want to.

"Or," said Max, "we could each put some glue in a paper cup!"

"Do you want to try that?" Jackie asked. We did. She smiled. "I'm proud of how you worked this problem out; it's not always easy to share."

What are some ways you cooperate with other kids?

I feel like sharing.

FEELING DIFFERENT

At circle time Jackie said she liked how well we were learning to share with one another. Then she asked, "Do you ever have things you don't want to share?"

We talked about things mommies and daddies don't share—like their watches or tools. Kevin was really quiet.

"How come Kevin never talks about his daddy?" asked Mandy.

Jackie said Kevin could share about his daddy if he wanted to. "It's up to Kevin," she said.

"Daddy doesn't live with us anymore," Kevin said softly, "I don't like it. I feel different."

Jackie said that there are all kinds of families. Your family is whoever loves you and takes care of you. Differences make us special.

We each thought of something special and different about our families.

What's special about your family?

I feel special.

HAPPY

Circle time was over. It was almost time to play outside.

I walked over to my cubby. I keep pictures of my mom and dad there. I smiled at them. Just then, Jackie called, "Let's get dressed for playing outside!"

I was the first one ready. "Guess what, Jackie!" I said. "I feel happy. I get to play outside and tonight we're going to have pizza for dinner!" I laughed and ran outside with Mandy.

There are many reasons to feel happy. What do you feel happy about?

I feel happy.

MAD

It was snowing outside. I ran over to the swings.

Suddenly, Mandy ran over, jumped on a swing, and crashed into me! I was MAD!

"Stop it, dummy!" I yelled. But she kept bumping me.

Jackie heard me. "Nathan, it's not okay to call someone a dummy. You sound upset. What happened?"

"She bumped me," I said loudly. "I don't like it. I told her to stop, but she did it again."

"I just wanted to play train with him," Mandy explained, "and he called me a dummy!"

"It's important to listen to one another and to be gentle with each other's bodies," said Jackie. "Mandy, can you think of a way to play train that doesn't hurt anyone? And Nathan, if Mandy doesn't listen, what else can you do?" she asked.

Mandy decided next time she can *ask* me to play.

I was glad I tried to use my words, but I sure got upset when they didn't work. Next time I'll ask Jackie for help.

Tell about what you did the last time you felt upset or mad at someone.

I feel mad.

CONCERN

Pretty soon, it was time for lunch. We had tacos. Yum, yum!

I sat down next to Max and Kevin. I saw Michael, the new boy, sitting all by himself. He looked lonely. I remembered how lonely I felt when I first came to Kids' Place. I thought everyone had a friend except me. One day, I started talking to Max about dinosaurs. Then I stopped feeling lonely. I felt happy to find a friend.

"Maybe Michael needs a friend," I thought. "Hey Max," I said, "let's go ask Michael if he likes dinosaurs."

"Sure," Max said.

Michael said he had lots of dinosaurs. We told him he could bring some for sharing at circle time. He smiled. Jackie was watching. She smiled too.

"You and Max were kind to Michael," she said.

When have you felt worried or concerned about someone else? What did you do?

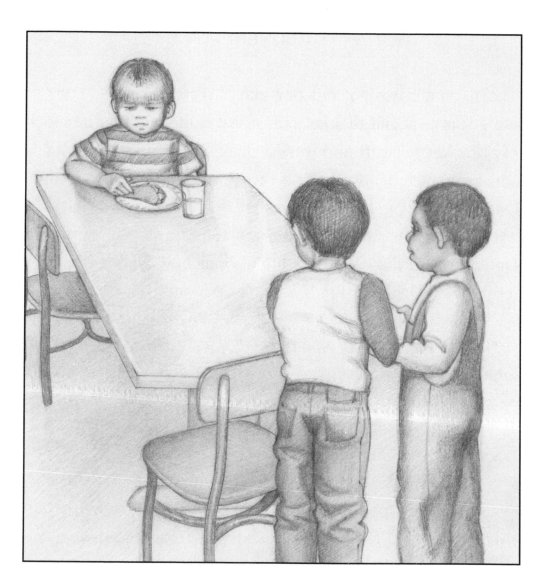

I feel concerned.

LOVE

After lunch, we got out our mats for naptime.

I got my special blanket out of my cubby and lay down. My blanket felt soft and warm. Jackie sang a sleepy song and gave each of us a hug. I thought about how Mom and Dad love me and how I love them.

I put my hand in my pocket and found a dinosaur picture Dad drew for me. When I think about how Dad loves me, I feel good. Dad says I'm a loveable person.

Do you ever think of someone you love when you're at school?

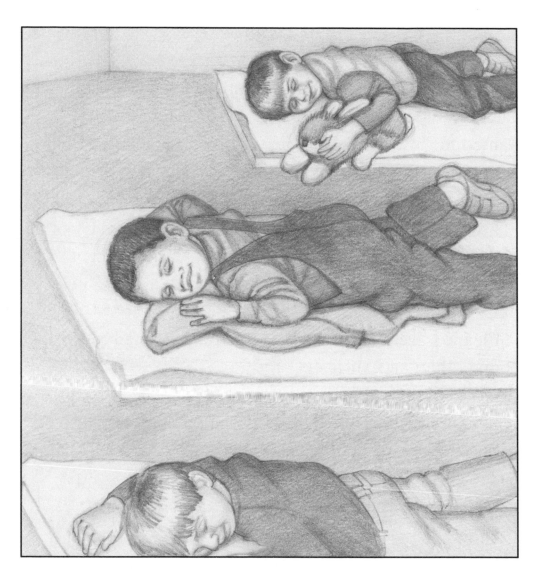

I feel loved.

REJECTED

Naptime was over. Jackie put on her magic storytelling hat. I wanted to sit next to Max, but he said "no." He wanted to sit with Michael. I felt sad and mad—I thought he was *my* friend! Everyone sat down but me.

"Find a seat, please, Nathan," Jackie said.

I told her I wanted to sit next to Max, but he said "no."

"It sounds like you're feeling left out," Jackie said. I nodded. I felt like crying and kind of mad at the same time.

I leaned over and pushed Max, hard. I wanted to get in between him and Michael.

"We don't push or hit people at Kids' Place," Jackie reminded me. "When *my* good friend pays attention to someone else, sometimes I feel rejected," she said. "That means feeling hurt and left out."

Max said he could sit in between Michael and me. I said "okay."

When have you felt rejected?

I feel rejected.

PROUD

Before I knew it, Mom came to get me. "I have a surprise, Mom!" I shouted. I felt so proud. I ran to get my picture. There were lots of other kids getting their pictures too. It was crowded.

Someone bumped into me and a feather fell off. I started to cry.

"Uh oh," said Mom. "I can see you worked hard on that. When we get home, we can glue the feather back on, if you'd like."

I thought about it. "No," I said. "I like it this way too. I made it 'specially for you." I felt proud again.

When do you feel proud of yourself? What do you say?

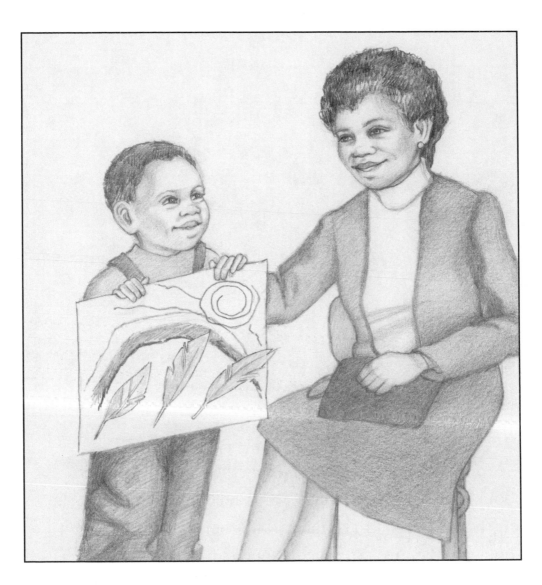

I feel proud.

Mom and I were glad to be together again. I talked about my day. I told about how I felt mixed up when she left, how I got mad at Mandy, and then how proud I felt about my picture. So much happened! Mom said she was glad I could tell her how I felt. She gave me a big hug as I got out of the car.

Survival Skills for Children in Childcare

More than the ABC's and 123's, children need to learn to emotionally negotiate the world of childcare. Parents and caregivers can help by recognizing and validating children's feelings and by keeping their social/emotional growth a priority.

Here are some additional language suggestions (we've used Nathan and his friends as examples) to guide children as they develop their own coping strategies in mastering these universal survival skills.

1. Compromise

Mandy had the swing first, but Nathan wants a chance to swing too. "Mandy, let's compromise. How about if you take ten more swings and then let Nathan have a turn, even though you were here first."

2. Empathy

"Kevin looks sad and might be feeling left out. Remember when you were new and felt lonely? I wonder if Kevin feels like that?"

3. Cooperation/Sharing/Taking Turns

"You sure know how to cooperate. You all shared the glue so everyone could work on their pictures, and you also took turns at snack time. Cooperating is more fun than fighting!"

4. Patience

"Waiting can be hard when you really want something. You can help yourself be patient. Can you find something or someone to play with while you wait?"

5. Flexibility

"I know you really want to be the only one to sit next to Max. Being flexible means wanting to do one thing, and then deciding to do something different."

6. Respect

"Respect means being gentle with each other's feelings and bodies and treating people like you want to be treated."

7. Negotiation

"Nathan, you can try asking Max if he'd like to trade toys or to let you know when he's finished. That's called negotiating for what you need. It doesn't always work, but we'll keep practicing, and we'll get better at it."

8. Disappointment

"Sometimes, as hard as we try, we don't always get what we want or need, and it doesn't feel fair. It can feel sad and disappointing. It's okay to feel that way. It happens to everyone, even grownups." (Try telling a story about a time when you didn't get what you needed and how it felt.)

9. Asking for Help

"I see how frustrated you are. It's okay to ask for help. People need each other."

10. Honesty

"I'm glad you were honest and told me the truth, even though you thought I would be mad at you."

Teach Children Social Skills!

The Children's Problem Solving books (second edition) by Elizabeth Crary help children learn social skills by letting them make decisions for the characters and then see the consequences.

These books are different! They are fun, game-like books, rather than traditional "sit-quiet" books. As one young child remarked to a friend, "You get to pick what happens. If you don't like what happened, you can go back and try again."

This series helps children **learn about feelings and behavior** in an easy, non-threatening way. The series *(32 pages, illus., 7 x 8½, $6.95 each)* includes:

I Want It: What can Amy do when Megan has the truck she wants?

I Can't Wait: How can Luke get a turn on the tumbling mat?

I Want To Play: How can Danny find someone to play with?

My Name Is Not Dummy: How can Jenny get Eduardo to stop calling her a dummy?

I'm Lost: What can Amy do to find her dad at the zoo?

Mommy, Don't Go: What can Matt do when he doesn't want his mother to leave?

FREE BOOK OFFER! Buy five problem solving books and get one free! A $41.70 value for only $34.75—order today!

All My Feelings at Home: Ellie's Day
By Susan Conlin and Susan Levine Friedman

Follow five-year-old Ellie throughout a day full of feelings. Children share with Ellie mixed feelings as she feels excited that friends are coming over to play, sad at the dead bird in the backyard, rejected when her friend won't play with her, happy at the thought of home-made ice cream, and more.

Grown-ups accept Ellie's feelings and guide her behavior when needed.
32 pages, 7 ½ x 8 ½ inches, $5.95 paperback, illustrated

Ask for these books at your favorite bookstore, or call 1-800-992-6657.
VISA and MasterCard accepted with telephone orders.
Complete book catalog available on request. Web site at www.ParentingPress.com

Parenting Press, Inc., Dept. 201, P.O. Box 75267, Seattle, WA 98125
In Canada, call **Raincoast Books Distribution Co.**, 1-800-663-5714
Prices subject to change without notice